This book is given with love:

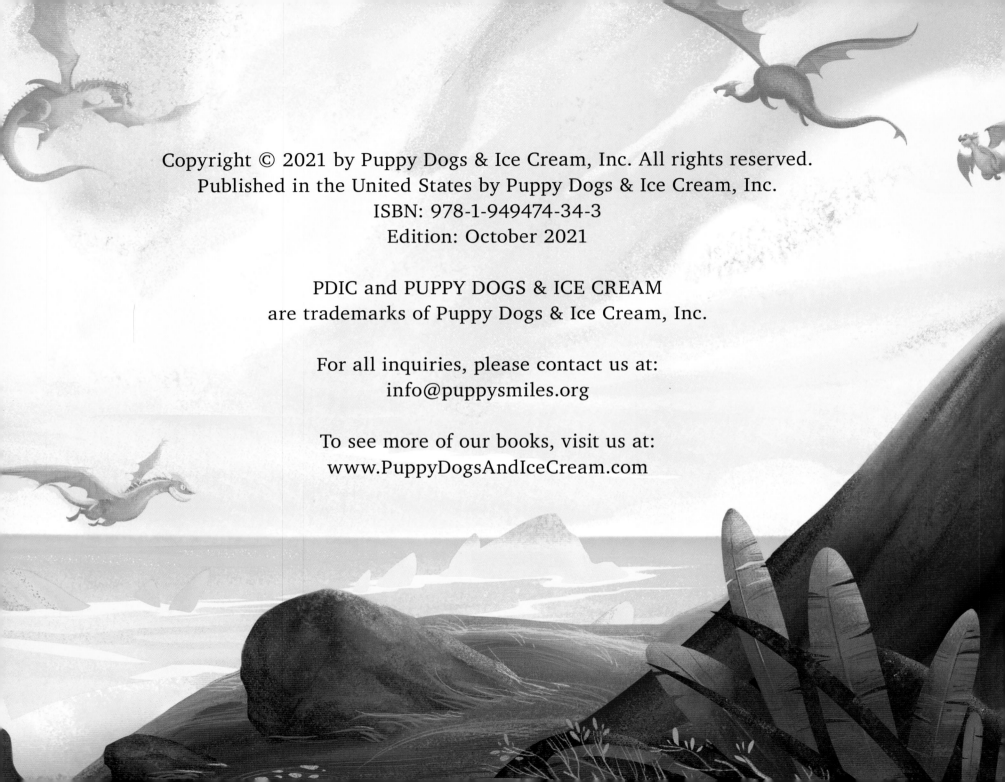

PDIC and PUPPY DOGS & ICE CREAM
are trademarks of Puppy Dogs & Ice Cream, Inc.

For all inquiries, please contact us at:
info@puppysmiles.org

To see more of our books, visit us at:
www.PuppyDogsAndIceCream.com

Pyra

A Story of Love, Patience & Hard Work

written by
Rachael Urrutia Chu

illustrated by
Ana Nguyen

Far, far away, past the highest clouds and the tallest mountains, beyond the wild winds and crashing seas, there lies a land of dragons...

They soar through the skies, let out mighty bellows of fire, climb over jagged cliffs, and dive deep into icy waters. But all dragons, big and small, were especially excited today... For, today, an egg was hatching!

The dragons gathered around the nest excitedly, watching the egg as it rumbled and cracked, until a little red dragon came tumbling out. They cheered and roared in a warm, dragon welcome as her mother's eyes filled with love. "Pyra", she cooed, "That is what your name shall be!"

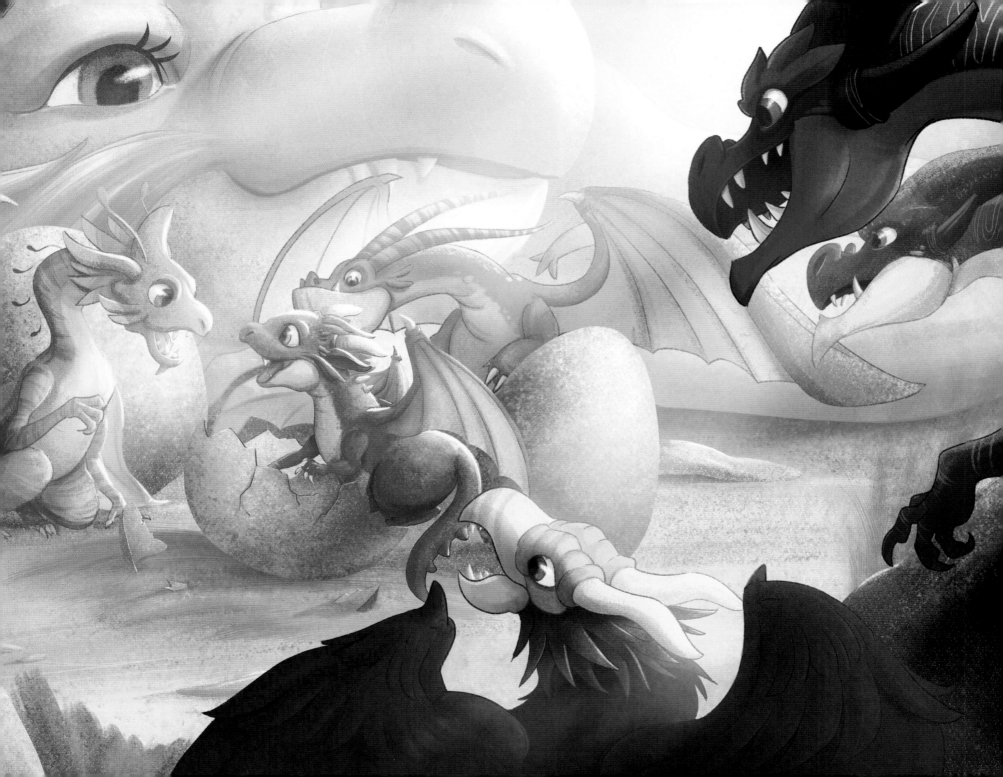

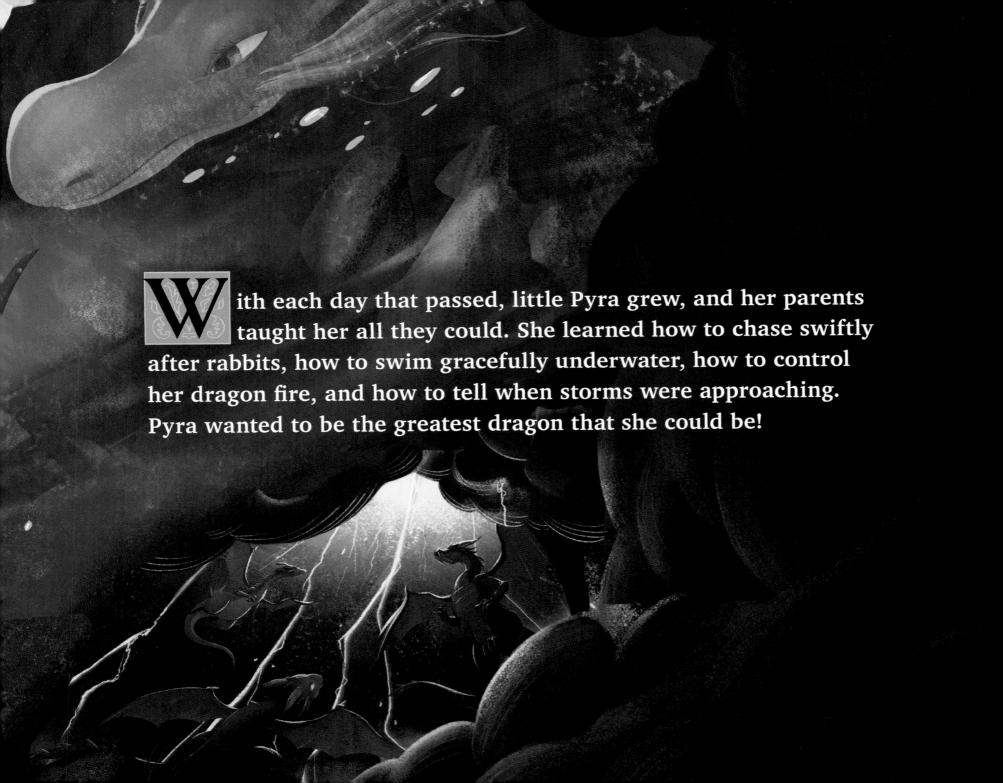

With each day that passed, little Pyra grew, and her parents taught her all they could. She learned how to chase swiftly after rabbits, how to swim gracefully underwater, how to control her dragon fire, and how to tell when storms were approaching. Pyra wanted to be the greatest dragon that she could be!

When she wasn't training, Pyra loved to play by the river with her friends. They were all eager to learn a dragon's greatest skill, flying. Each of them wanted to be the first to fly, but it all depended on who could "find the wind" first.

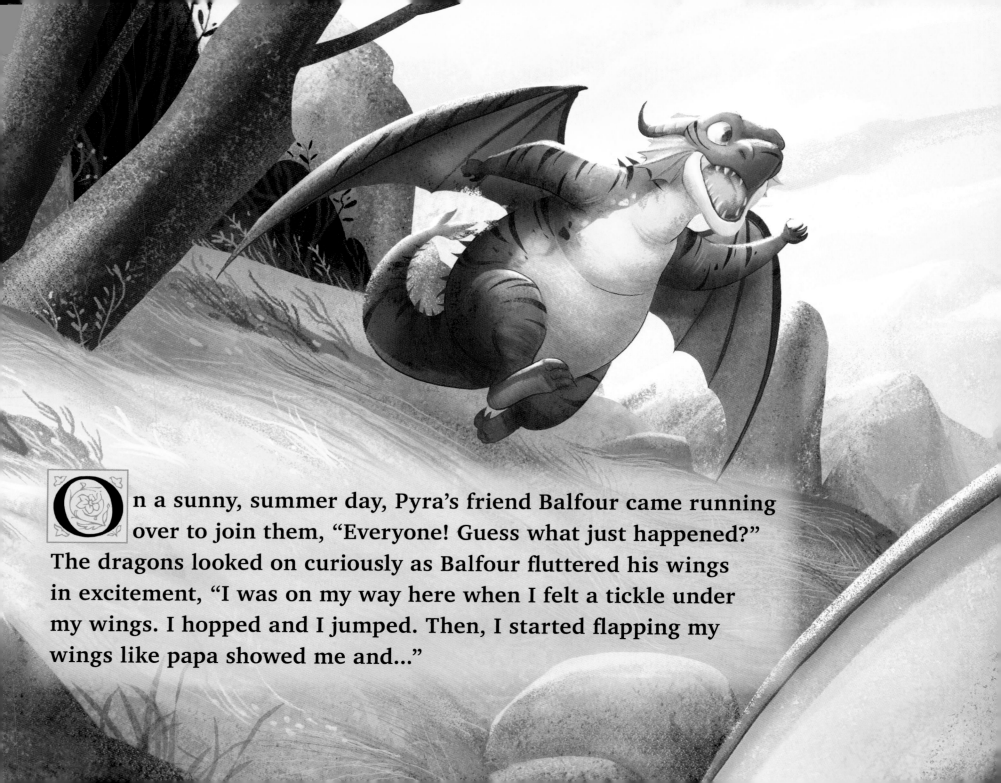

On a sunny, summer day, Pyra's friend Balfour came running over to join them, "Everyone! Guess what just happened?" The dragons looked on curiously as Balfour fluttered his wings in excitement, "I was on my way here when I felt a tickle under my wings. I hopped and I jumped. Then, I started flapping my wings like papa showed me and..."

The purple dragon then leapt into the air, flapping his wings as hard as he could. He struggled at first, but was soon soaring high above his friends. The young dragons cheered, "Hooray, Balfour! You did it! You're flying!"

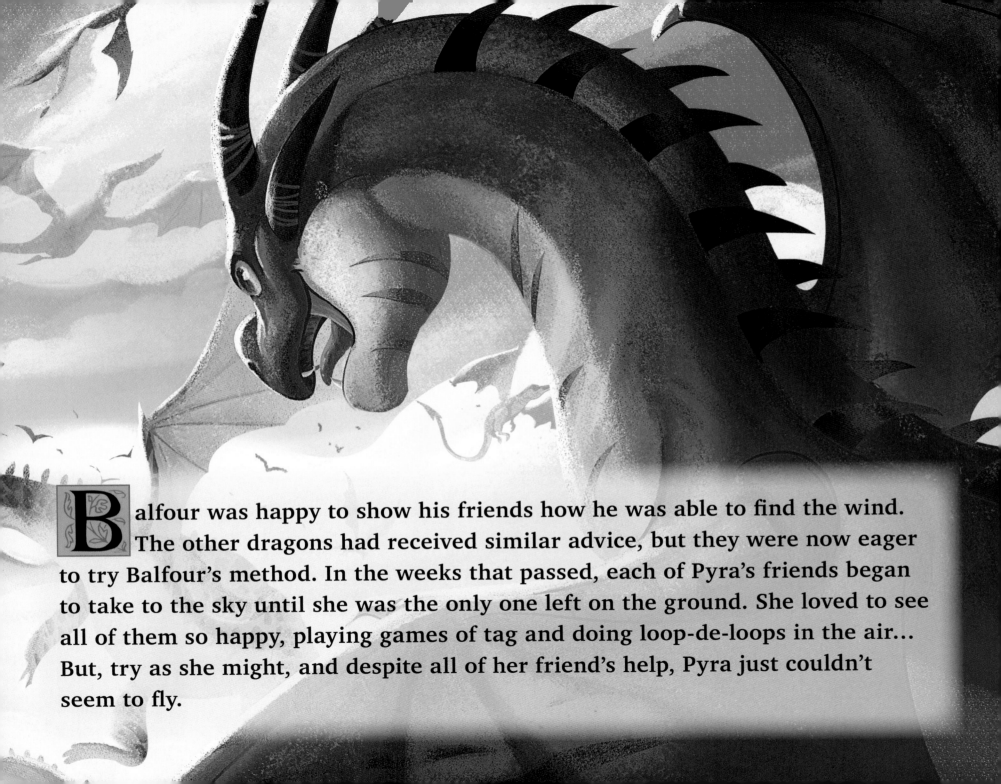

Balfour was happy to show his friends how he was able to find the wind. The other dragons had received similar advice, but they were now eager to try Balfour's method. In the weeks that passed, each of Pyra's friends began to take to the sky until she was the only one left on the ground. She loved to see all of them so happy, playing games of tag and doing loop-de-loops in the air... But, try as she might, and despite all of her friend's help, Pyra just couldn't seem to fly.

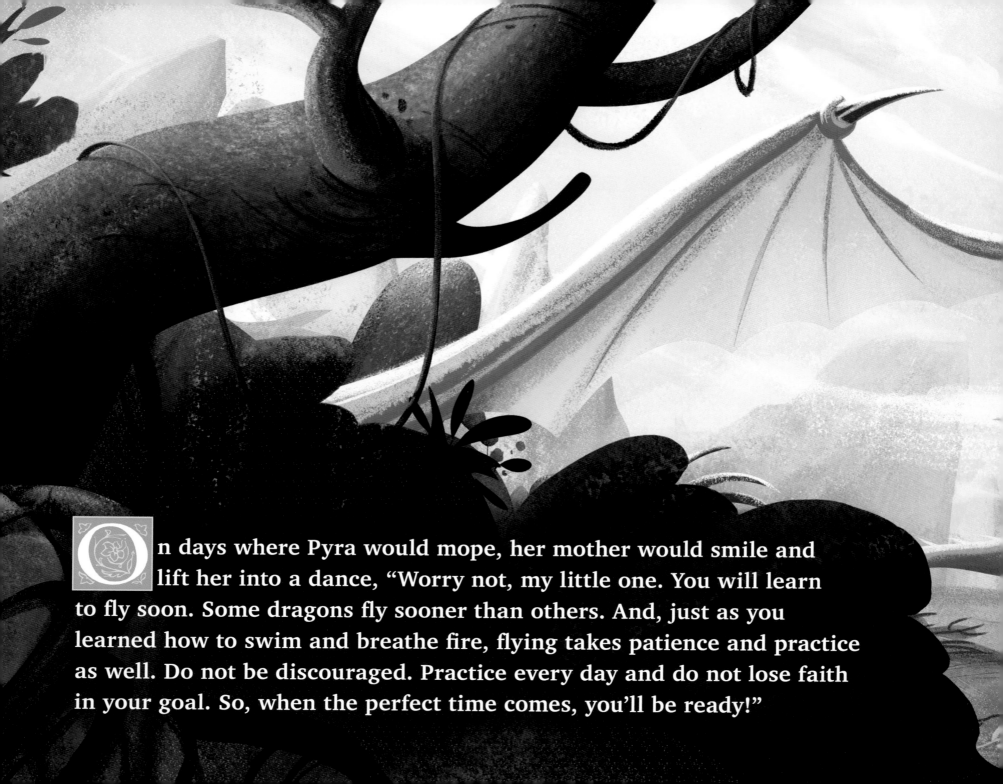

On days where Pyra would mope, her mother would smile and lift her into a dance, "Worry not, my little one. You will learn to fly soon. Some dragons fly sooner than others. And, just as you learned how to swim and breathe fire, flying takes patience and practice as well. Do not be discouraged. Practice every day and do not lose faith in your goal. So, when the perfect time comes, you'll be ready!"

Pyra was determined to find the wind that would help her fly. She practiced every day, leaping into the air and flapping her wings anytime she felt the slightest breeze. Pyra even tried asking the older dragons how they learned to fly and did what they suggested. But, after each attempt, all she was met with was a face full of dirt and grass…

Watching her friends frolic in the clouds above, Pyra let out a big sigh. She was trying so hard and wanted to fly so badly. Pyra was sure she wanted it more than anyone else! But still, she did not succeed. More than once, the thought crossed her mind that she might never learn how to fly, and today was no different... With tears in her eyes, she hung her head low and sulked home to her mother.

"Mama, will you love me even if I never learn to fly?" asked Pyra sadly. Her mother smiled and gave her a hug, "Of course, Pyra. I will love you no matter what. I know failing is not fun, and waiting can be frustrating, but wouldn't it be a shame to give up after trying so many times? You also learned something each time you failed, didn't you? You fluttered a bit higher, glided a bit farther, and got a bit stronger. I can see you're almost there. Give it more time and do not give up!"

Her mother was right. She couldn't give up! With a smile and a nod, Pyra kissed her mother's cheek and ran off to try flying again. Finding a nice grassy hill, the little red dragon took a deep breath before running as fast as she could into the wind. With a flit, flutter, and flap, Pyra soon felt a strange tickle under her wings...

She was suddenly moving quickly through the fields, faster than she ever had before! The wind was whipping around Pyra as she continued to flap her wings. And, looking down to her feet, she saw they weren't touching the ground anymore! "I did it!" Pyra cheered, "I'm flying!"

The little red dragon smiled and zoomed higher into sky, looking down at the island that she called home. She had found the wind when she least expected it, on a day just like any other. She had taken everyone's advice on what to do. She had practiced every day. And – most importantly – she didn't give up!

The wind felt amazing as it rushed past her face and under her wings. Pyra now felt like she could do anything! Looking ahead, she saw the familiar forms of her friends and zoomed over to them with a twist and a twirl. Finally, she could join them in the sky!

Calling over to Balfour, he looked at Pyra with surprise.
A great, big grin then came over his face. "Look who's flying!"
Balfour exclaimed as he waved over to her, "I knew you could do it, Pyra!"
The two friends laughed together as they glided through the air and
soon met up with the others.

The dragons roared and cheered as they saw their friend flying. They were happy for her, since they knew how long and hard she had practiced. The friends flew in the sky for hours. They talked about the games they could play and offered advice on how Pyra could become even better at flying. When evening came, Pyra said goodbye and raced back home. She couldn't wait to tell her parents the good news!

From that day on, Pyra continued to grow and became a big, strong, and beautiful dragon. It seemed like just yesterday that she was struggling to find the wind. But now? She could soar in the sky with such ease! And it was all thanks to the support of everyone around her, telling her not to give up and to have patience.

Pyra took every chance she could to help young dragons whenever they were struggling. She would gather the little dragons together and offer them the lessons she had learned so long ago. "Look at you all, so different and unique! Just like the journeys we all take… Some challenges in life will be harder than others. Sometimes we need to step back from a problem and look at it from a new angle or seek advice before trying again. Failing can be discouraging, but we grow and learn something new with each attempt. Failure is merely a stepping stone towards your goal."

Each time she taught her lessons, Pyra could see determination rise up in the young dragons. One by one, they each overcame their challenges in their own time and would share Pyra's words of inspiration, "Have patience, practice, and – most importantly – never give up!"

🐾 Claim Your FREE Gift! 🐾

Visit ➡ PDICBooks.com/Gift

Thank you for purchasing Pyra,
and welcome to the Puppy Dogs & Ice Cream family.

We're certain you're going to love the little gift
we've prepared for you at the website above.